# Blown Away: A Fall Adventure

Taswya Anthony

AuthorHouse™
1663 Liberty Drive
Bloomington, IN 47403
www.authorhouse.com
Phone: 833-262-8899

This book is printed on acid-free paper.

ISBN: 979-8-8230-3782-2 (sc)
ISBN: 979-8-8230-3783-9 (e)

Library of Congress Control Number: 2024923817

Print information available on the last page.

Published by AuthorHouse 11/07/2024

authorHOUSE®

# Blown Away: A Fall Adventure

"Jambo, Zulu!" shouted Baba Shabazz with a warm smile. "Jambo!" whispered the little ones as they shuffled into the classroom, ready for the day's morning circle.

As Baba Shabazz reviewed the calendar and weather with the class in Zulu, the excitement in the room was palpable. "Who can tell me what today is?" he asked.
"It's Monday!" said Aniyah.
"Great job, Aniyah!" Baba Shabazz praised. "And what's the date?"
"It's the 21st!" Khy said proudly.

"Excellent observation, Khy! And what month are we in?"
"October!" the class chimed together.
"Amazing!" Baba Shabazz continued. "And what season are we in?"
"Fall!" Nia raised her hand and answered. "It gets very windy in fall and it can blow us away."
The little ones giggled at the thought. Miles shook his head, "The wind can't blow people away. That's silly."

4

"Alright, Zulu Class, it's time to put on our sweaters and jackets," Baba Shabazz said. "Let's go for a neighborhood walk to collect leaves!"

As the class set out on their walk, they noticed the leaves on the ground were swirling and dancing in the wind. The breeze grew stronger, and soon the children called out, "Baba Shabazz! Baba Shabazz! Some of our friends have blown away!"

The group counted quickly. There were only 6 little ones on the line. "How many are missing?" asked Baba Shabazz.

"Four!" Kyrie and Mya shouted.

"Right!" Baba Shabazz nodded. "We need to find our four missing friends."

The Zulu Class walked down Smith Street, searching high and low.

8

They spotted Jabari stuck in a tree. Baba Shabazz helped Jabari climb down safely.

Next, they heard calls for help coming from another but taller tree. Shaun and Isabella had been blown onto the branches of a tree ! The firefighters quickly came to the rescue, using their ladder to save the children one by one.

"Thank you, firefighters!" the little ones cheered.

"Now let's find our last friend," Baba Shabazz said, leading the way. They walked down Maple Street, searching for Karter.

After a thorough search, they finally spotted him, hidden inside a giant pile of leaves. "Come on, guys! Jump in!" Karter called out.

The little ones, including Baba Shabazz, leaped into the leaf pile, laughing and playing joyfully.

14

After a while, Baba Shabazz gathered everyone together. "It's time to head back to school and get ready for lunch."

With all the little ones safely on the line, they walked back to the school.

Ding! Ding! Ding! The naptime timer buzzed, and Nia woke up from her cot. She smiled and chuckled, "Haha, blow me away! That's silly. It was just a dream!"

The Zulu Class shared a hearty laugh and looked forward to their next adventure, real or imagined.

Printed in the United States
by Baker & Taylor Publisher Services